Snap books ™

The World of Fashion

1

Fashion
CAREERS

Finding the
Right Fit

by Jen Jones

1

Consultant: Lindsay Stewart
Director of the Children's Division
Jet Set Models
La Jolla, California

Capstone
press ®
Mankato, Minnesota

Snap Books are published by Capstone Press,
151 Good Counsel Drive, P.O. Box 669, Mankato, Minnesota 56002.
www.capstonepress.com

Library of Congress Cataloging-in-Publication Data
Jones, Jen, 1976–
    Fashion careers: finding the right fit / by Jen Jones.
    p. cm.—(Snap books. The World of fashion)
    Summary: "Explains various fashion careers and the skills and
experience needed for them"—Provided by publisher.
    Includes bibliographical references and index.
    ISBN-13: 978-0-7368-6829-7 (hardcover)
    ISBN-10: 0-7368-6829-1 (hardcover)
    ISBN-13: 978-0-7368-7883-8 (softcover pbk.)
    ISBN-10: 0-7368-7883-1 (softcover pbk.)
    1. Fashion—Vocational guidance—Juvenile literature. 2. Clothing
trade—Vocational guidance—Juvenile literature. I. Title. II. Series.
TT507.J663 2007
746.9'2023—dc22
                                      2006021845

Editor: Amber Bannerman
Designer: Juliette Peters
Photo Researcher: Charlene Deyle

Photo Credits:
Capstone Press/TJ Thoraldson Digital Photography, 24; Corbis/LWA-Stephen Welstead, 12 (bottom); Corbis/Paul A.
Souders, 19; Corbis/Paul Barton, cover (left), 9; Corbis/ZUMA/Petre Buzoianu, 27; Getty Images Inc./Iconica/Simon
Wilkinson, 13; Getty Images Inc./The Image Bank/Marc Romanelli, 15; Getty Images Inc./The Image Bank/M Nader,
25; Getty Images Inc./Marsaili McGrath, 23; Getty Images Inc./Peter Kramer, 20; Getty Images Inc./Stone/Robert Daly,
7; Getty Images Inc./Stone/Ryan McVay, 21; Getty Images Inc./Taxi/Antonio Mo, 5; Getty Images Inc./Taxi/Martin
Riedl, 17 (left); Getty Images Inc./Taxi/Paul Viant, 29; The Image Works/Larry Mangino, 17 (right); Michele Torma Lee,
32; PhotoEdit Inc./Michael Newman, 11; Shutterstock/Andres Rodriguez, 18; Shutterstock/Jenny Solomon, 12 (top);
Shutterstock/Marek Walica, 4; Shutterstock/Mares Lucian, 10; Shutterstock/Michael Ledray, 26; Shutterstock/Sebastian
Kaulitzki, 22; Shutterstock/Stephen Coburn, cover (right); Shutterstock/Teodor Ostojic, 28

1 2 3 4 5 6 12 11 10 09 08 07

Table of Contents

Inside the Industry

Are you dying to try on a fashion career for size? You're not alone. It's hard not to be drawn in by designer labels and supermodel smiles. But did you know the fashion industry is more than just a pretty face? Many people work together behind the scenes. They use their skills to create clothing that customers will want. It's just like a carefully sewn shirt. If one thread comes loose, a whole project could come undone.

In this book, you'll learn about many fashion careers. Whether you want to rock the retail floor or sketch sassy designs, you'll find the tools you need. Prepare to explore the many faces of fashion!

The Right Fit

Moving up in the fashion world isn't easy. Thousands of hungry graduates enter the field every year. Many of them are competing for the same jobs. This makes it tough to get even the fanciest foot in the door. In the end, success comes to those with talent, strong business contacts, and a unique vision.

Wondering if you've got what it takes? A career in fashion might be the right fit if you . . .

- constantly have your nose buried in fashion magazines.

- dream of living in a big city.

- aren't afraid to try a new look.

- are a pro at sewing or drawing.

- have a combination of business smarts and cutting-edge creativity.

- have a passion for fashion!

Chapter One

The Creation of Clothing: Every Role Counts

Are Textiles Your Style?

Are you a material girl who flips for fabric? If so, you might find a future in textiles. Textiles are the materials used to make clothes. They determine the look, feel, and weight of what we wear.

Mission Possible: Jobs You Can Do

Thousands of textile designs exist. They range from paisley to pinstripes. *Textile designers* dream up these patterns and prints. Their ideas make pieces of clothing special. *CAD designers* use computers to create textile masterpieces, while other textile designers work by hand. Whether using technology or paper, all designers must be skilled artists with an eye for color.

Textile designers work closely with *colorists* and *stylists*. Colorists suggest new color combinations. They must know whether to "think pink" or go "true blue." Stylists guide a clothing line's creative direction.

Designing Divas

When a *fashion designer* sketches an idea, a new piece of clothing is born! To see the light of day, a clothing idea goes through a long process. Its path goes from design to production to sale. The people behind the pencils are very important. They plant the creative seeds for daring dresses and stylish shirts.

Mission Possible: Jobs You Can Do

Many categories exist within the fashion industry. Among them are men's, women's, children's, and accessories. (Not to mention swimwear and sleepwear.) Yet landing a job can be hard. There are currently only about 17,000 fashion designers in the United States. To make the hiring cut, a fashion designer must have many talents. She needs determination, endless ideas, and great garment-making skills.

Mad About Manufacturing

During manufacturing, fabric pieces make the leap to the finished product. In the factories, many hands are needed to get the job done. Like pieces in a puzzle, each worker plays a big part in the final product.

Mission Possible: Jobs You Can Do

Spreaders and *cutters* prepare fabric for the sewing machine operators. After checking the fabric for flaws, they cut it into shapes that are stitched together.

Sewing machine operators make up more than half of the employees in the apparel industry. They work the large machines that join the pieces of clothing together.

Costing engineers decide how a company can best divide its money. They figure out how much materials and labor will cost for any given project.

Seamstresses and *tailors* are sewing whizzes who create and alter clothing. They do things like sew sequins to a dress, hem a skirt, or add zippers.

Industrial engineers find the smartest ways to use available time, resources, and money to produce the best possible clothes.

Production managers watch over the factory floor. They supervise each employee and the overall process.

Clothing's Crystal Ball

Did you think the bohemian look was the next big thing long before it really was? If so, you've got a talent for predicting trends. New clothing lines are entering the market constantly. Never before have trend-spotters been so important to a company's success.

Mission Possible: Jobs You Can Do

Fashion forecasters must know fashion's past, present, and future. They guess what will be "hot" or "not" in coming years. Also hot on the trail for up-and-coming looks are *trend analysts*. They give advice to production teams on popular colors and cuts.

Merchandisers also follow market trends. A merchandiser's main goal is to improve a company's profitability. A merchandiser might look at past successful items and sales figures to guide a new "Back to School" clothing line.

Chapter Two

Onto the Racks: Those Who Help Others Dress to Impress

A Head for Wholesale

When shopping, it's very common to see many identical items for sale. This is because the store buys clothing in bulk, or wholesale. Lots of behind-the-scenes work goes on to get the clothes to the retail rack. *Wholesale workers* are the wizards behind the curtain!

Mission Possible: Jobs You Can Do

The designer showroom is where the wholesale magic happens. New products are presented there for the first time. A *showroom manager* makes pretty displays for the new merchandise. She also keeps an eye on showroom operations.

Buyers just might have the most power in the business. These decision-makers visit showrooms to meet with sales representatives. Each season, they view the new clothing lines and decide what will be sold in stores. Next time you see a sassy skirt or a cute swimsuit on the rack, you'll know a buyer was behind it!

17

Retail: Great Fashion Unveiled

Unlike wholesale workers, retail workers are much more visible. They work "on the floor" of about 150,000 clothing stores nationwide. From quirky boutiques to busy department stores, the retail industry serves and clothes the public. And it's clear the public is hungry for fashion. The average American adult buys 52 pieces of clothing each year!

Mission Possible: Jobs You Can Do

Many roles make a retail store go round. At the top of the list is the *store owner*. She is the driving force behind the operation. A store must also have *salespeople*, *cashiers*, and *managers*. These employees help customers and keep the business running smoothly.

Ever go window-shopping and wonder who designs those dazzling displays? *Visual display artists* artfully create window and in-store displays. Their creations are meant to attract customers and show clothes in their best light.

Media Moguls

In the pages of *Vogue* and other magazines, fashion comes alive. Models pose in beautiful designer creations. Magazines and other media have a big impact on the fashions we buy and admire. A company's sales often rise after a photo spread showcases its items. Celebrity fashion ads and photos also influence our choices.

Mission Possible:
Jobs You Can Do

Because magazines reach so many readers, *magazine editors* can sway buying decisions. They select the designers and clothes that will be featured on the publication's pages.

Vogue *magazine editors attending fashion show*

Photographers are the talent behind the lens. They snap shots of fashion models, bringing life to the fab fashions.

Creativity is key for *copywriters* and *advertising professionals*. They create snappy slogans and eye-catching ads. They aim to set a brand apart from the rest.

It's all about positive spin for *public relations specialists*. They work tirelessly to spread the word about new products.

21

Playing Dress-Up

Do you mentally make over strangers? If you want to help the fashion-challenged, you'd make a great style expert. These trend-setters know how to choose flattering colors and fits. From suiting up stars to shopping galore, glamour is the name of the game!

Mission Possible: Jobs You Can Do

Imagine getting paid to go shopping! *Personal shoppers* do just that. They take stock of a person's likes and dislikes in order to select new clothing. *Wardrobe consultants* are paid to transform a client's image. They know how to change looks from punk to proper or stuffy to sassy.

Celebrity wardrobe stylist Rachel Zoe

Watch any red carpet event. Turn the pages of *US Weekly*. You'll see celebs sporting the latest looks from the hottest designers. *Wardrobe stylists* are the people who seek out these pricey, stylish items for the stars. Wardrobe stylists also are hired for photo shoots.

Chapter Three

A Passion for Fashion: Picking Your Path

Getting Suited for Success

Although you probably have a few years of school left, you can update your fashion industry smarts now. When it comes to fashion, you can never be too informed. Attending local fashion shows is a great sneak peek at how things work. Reading magazines will also keep your style smarts up-to-date. When doing your "homework," cut out pictures that inspire you. As your collection grows, your personal style will take shape.

As you get older, you can put your fashion career on the fast track. Many colleges offer fashion-related degrees. Apprenticeships allow young designers to work closely with successful designers. Internships let students earn school credit while working for a company.

Climbing the Ladder

Many famous designers launched their careers with low-paying, no-glory jobs. For instance, designer Marc Jacobs started out working in the stockroom of a New York clothing store. There he met designer Perry Ellis. Later in life, Jacobs designed collections for Ellis' company. Today, Jacobs' self-titled clothing is sold in many upscale stores.

Designer Marc Jacobs at a fashion show in 2004

Stories like this teach an important lesson. Paying your dues can pay off. Smart beginners also know that it's important to network. Becoming familiar with trade associations such as the American Apparel and Footwear Association (AAFA) makes it easy to meet others in "the biz." Use these keys to success to open the door of opportunity!

Landing the
Real Thing

Imagine a giant walk-in closet filled with clothes. The fashion world is much like that closet. Jobs exist for everyone from artists to accountants. Many people go for exciting career choices like modeling or fashion design. But don't forget that hundreds of jobs lie under the industry's shiny surface.

While getting a job in fashion may seem far in the future, you can start getting involved now. Learning to sew or knit can give you great garment-making practice. Getting a job at stores like Limited Too or Aeropostale will show you how the retail side works. By the time you're ready to go professional, you'll be an old pro!

alter (AWL-tur)—to slightly change a clothing article

boutique (boo-TEEK)—a small unique store

bulk (BUHLK)—a large amount

CAD (CAD)—abbreviation for computer-aided design

degree (di-GREE)—proof of graduating from college

network (NET-wurk)—to talk with others in the same industry to make connections

slogan (SLOH-guhn)—a catchphrase or motto

textile (TEK-stile)—fabric or cloth that is created by weaving or knitting

Fast Facts

Twin fashionistas Mary-Kate and Ashley Olsen have their own ultra-successful retail company called Dualstar. Tweens and teens sweep through retail store doors, hungry for the company's clothing, make-up, and other products. The company has raked in about $1 billion.

If you see a sassy sandal with a red sole, it might be one of Christian Louboutin's creations. His luxury designs are easily spotted by their red soles.

Giorgio Armani holds the Guinness World Record for being the world's highest-paid fashion designer. In 1999, he set the record, earning a cool $135 million!

McAlpine, Margaret. *Working in the Fashion Industry.* My Future Career. Milwaukee: Gareth Stevens, 2006.

Rivera, Ursula. *Fashion.* American Pop Culture. New York: Children's Press, 2004.

Wallner, Rosemary. *Fashion Designer.* Career Exploration. Mankato, Minn.: Capstone Press, 2001.

Internet Sites

FactHound offers a safe, fun way to find Internet sites related to this book. All of the sites on FactHound have been researched by our staff.

Here's how:
1. Visit *www.facthound.com*
2. Choose your grade level.
3. Type in this book ID **0736868291** for age-appropriate sites. You may also browse subjects by clicking on letters, or by clicking on pictures and words.
4. Click on the **Fetch It** button.

FactHound will fetch the best sites for you!

About the Author

Jen Jones has always been fascinated by fashion—and the evidence can be found in her piles of magazines and overflowing closet! She is a Los Angeles-based writer who has published stories in magazines such as *American Cheerleader*, *Dance Spirit*, *Ohio Today*, and *Pilates Style*. She has also written for E! Online and PBS Kids. Jones has been a Web site producer for *The Jenny Jones Show*, *The Sharon Osbourne Show*, and *The Larry Elder Show*. She's also written books for young girls on cheerleading, knitting, figure skating, and gymnastics.

Index